Before being a teacher, the author was once a student, who wrote short stories.
Now, he writes short stories as well as novels, and has a novel titled, *"A Piece of Fabric – Sahar"*

I dedicate the first part of these stories to Austin Macauley Publishers for helping me get my stories published, and the remaining to my beloved sisters, who always support me.

Khalid Bin Khalifa Al-Qanbar

13 SINS

WHY 13?

AUSTIN MACAULEY PUBLISHERS™
LONDON • CAMBRIDGE • NEW YORK • SHARJAH

Copyright © Khalid Bin Khalifa Al-Qanbar 2022

The right of Khalid Bin Khalifa Al-Qanbar to be identified as author of this work has been asserted by the author in accordance with Federal Law No. (7) of UAE, Year 2002, Concerning Copyrights and Neighboring Rights.

All rights reserved. No part of this publication may be reproduced, stored in a retrieval system, or transmitted in any form or by any means, electronic, mechanical, photocopying, recording, or otherwise, without the prior permission of the publishers.

Any person who commits any unauthorized act in relation to this publication may be liable to legal prosecution and civil claims for damages.

The age group that matches the content of the books has been classified according to the age classification system issued by the National Media Council.

ISBN – 9789948041610 – (Paperback)
ISBN – 9789948041627– (E-Book)

Application Number: MC-10-01-9954800
Age Classification: 17+

Printer Name: iPrint Global Ltd
Printer Address: Witchford, England

First Published 2022
AUSTIN MACAULEY PUBLISHERS FZE
Sharjah Publishing City
P.O Box [519201]
Sharjah, UAE
www.austinmacauley.ae
+971 655 95 202

I would like to thank those who read these stories and envisage them.

Love Besieged

Prologue

Wars are plotted by world's leaders, paid for by world's populations.

2005, Aleppo, Syria

A city known for its breathtaking nature that attracts tourists due to its magnificent designs and structures, let alone the benevolence of its people.

A love story was born among the suburbs between Samy; the 18-year-old brilliant graduate of high school, who was enrolled for mandatory military service in his county, and Sham; the wide, blue-eyed, graceful and tall young lady.

Earlier in 2003, before the so-called "Arab Spring" and within the context of events taking place in North Africa, world's leaders were falling like autumn leaves due to their tyranny upon the orders of their nations. In wars, the tenacious are the first to retreat. That's life. *"Such days (of varying fortunes) We give to men and men by turns." (Holy Quran)*

The eyes of the lovers were observing the scene of the Arab region as well as of their own country, into which invaders and terrorist groups stormed. Families either fled and left their cities and villages behind or stood still. Sham and Samy's were amongst those who stood still.

Under the horrifying sounds of blasts and airplane raids conducted by the Syrian regime, buildings were brought down and terrorist groups started to kidnap the Syrians. Cities collapsed and were taken over by the mighty regime.

Various groups were fighting, amongst which, some fought for liberation, while others were trying to get back in control. Other groups were mere terrorists. Aleppo remained under siege while both families stood still and together, they shared a house.

Sham's father lost his life in a suicide bombing in Aleppo market leaving behind a family in grief. Samy tried to help the family lessen such grief; he used to bring both the needs of both families.

Days passed by and turned into months and years till Sham was kidnapped by an ISIS terrorist group. Usually, such groups either turn their trophies of women into maids or wives. Sham had once made a promise to Samy that no man's hand should lay on her body but his!

Women were kept in house under the control of terrorists, who failed to turn Sham into either version. So, they raped her, bruised her, and finally she became the maid they sought her to be.

Samy was burning in agony; he wanted to get his beloved back before they killed her or worse! He started to contact all terrorist groups and even bribed some of them to get a tip.

Moreover, Samy joined an ISIS group; not to fight on their side, but he simply wanted to free his girl. He grew his fair-haired beard and became a militant, who killed people and vandalized property after his brain was washed. Later, he forgot about his goal and what he had been looking for.

It was time to distribute trophies, including Sham. She seemed different; her face was not the same anymore, hunger and violence showed more of her cheekbones. Samy could not recognize her, but he picked her up for his trophy and ordered her to step into his room. They got in and he wanted to rape her.

"Stop it, please, Samy," she shouted.

"Who do you mean?!" he asked.

She told him whom she meant. She meant Samy; the vigorous man, who helped them during the times of war. The one who supported the family following the death of its guardian and fought those who wanted to kidnap her

"Is that you, Sham!?" the terrorist wept.

"How did you know my name?" she wondered.

"It's me! Samy, your love," he replied.

They hugged tightly, but he almost forgot that they were in the house of terrorists! How could they run away?!

He made a plan and set a trap; starting with planting explosives around the room with a string tied to the door, once the door opened, the room would blow up, killing terrorists inside. Samy and Sham fled through the window, carrying a gun to defend themselves.

He headed to northern Syria reaching for Turkey. Hearing the sounds of a huge explosion coming from the village, where terrorists were hiding, Samy ran away. Bullets and grenades were heard all over the place as the Russian air force headed to the explosion point. The village was bombarded and silence filled the air.

Samy shaved his beard and his face became more familiar to Sham, who was over cloud nine.

Samy and Sham made it to Turkey, where they were approved to get in the country and placed with a group of refugees.

The next step was to look for their families. They spent hours looking till they found them. Sham's family kept thanking Samy for saving their daughter, then they parted again; however, their eyes did not.

The Next Morning...

Samy pulled himself together, got rid of his bashfulness, and told his father about his intentions to marry Sham. Immediately, the father agreed and headed to ask for her hand in marriage.

Sham's mother entered into her daughter's tent to bring her the good news; however, Sham was quiet and silent, it seemed that all the agony she had gone through had taken away her spirit and soul, leaving her family in distress and Samy in tears for losing his love, who was alive yet soulless.

May Allah keep all his believers safe and sound!

Part One
113 Gypsies

Prologue

Man may sense things in his life, yet they remain intangible to him, such as, ghosts, nightmares, and jinn.

It was a village inhabited by 113 gypsies. The sounds made by those gypsies in the middle of the night made the village seem as if haunted by ghosts. They used to play bizarre musical instruments…but why?!

Lojain was a journalist known for her exclusive reports. She had that tendency to reach places before everyone else. How did she do it?!

One day, Lojain heard about the gypsies' village and wanted to get more details about their lifestyle; how they lived and who was their chief.

Lojain rushed into the woods and with each step she took, she could hear the scary music getting louder. She wanted to reach the village before it got dark. In a glance, a ghost passed her by and left her in terror.

"Oh my god, help me!" she screamed.

A hand reached her from behind and tapped her back. It was the hand of a gypsy.

"Do not worry! You have made it to our village. This way, please." The gypsy guided her.

On the way to the village, they introduced themselves. Reaching their destination, all the gypsies gathered around Lojain, who immediately announced her wish to meet with the village chief. The villagers told her that they did not have such a thing. Lojain wondered how a village with such number of inhabitants lacked a chief and waited until midnight, when the scary music she once heard in the woods started again. The sounds were made by all the gypsies, but she could not understand what it meant or what it was about.

"What are these sounds for?" Lojain asked.

All of a sudden, a rough-haired man with two horns hanging over his head and a long tail showed up while holding a reap hook in his hand. All the gypsies howled and fell to their knees.

"Bring me this girl as a sacrifice and I shall stay away from you!" the man mumbled.

The scene was too difficult to bear, Lojain lost her consciousness and missed the following scene after the appearance of such a creature.

When she got her senses back, she could not find the creature; however, she found a human body cut into seven parts hanging over a group of trees. Interestingly, the human body was bloodless; the creature had sucked its blood, leaving the body behind for crows and other birds of prey to feed on the next day.

Lojain sought to know what had happened. One of the gypsies briefed her, but she could not believe what she heard. She asked them about that creature, but they could not even utter its name!

Lojain went back to her city to put her story in the newspaper she was working for to have a new exclusive.

However, she could not remember anything about that incident, which became foggy to her memory.

She went back to the place, where the village had been, but she could not find anyone. They were all gone!

She remembered that the gypsies are always on the road followed by that creature, wherever they went!

End of Part One

A Tip:

Always read "*Mu'awwizatain*" aka the "Verses of Refugee" before going to bed as you never know what dreams you may have or which ghosts you may see.

Part Two
113 Gypsies

Prologue

God has planted goodness in his creation; however, evilness is the result of the envy and hatred shown by those creatures. An introduction for certain people to get!

As Lojain was out of her consciousness, things had changed. But she did not know anything about them. She could not even remember such things as cutting the human body into parts. Why did she lose all this information right after she woke up?!

Let me tell you what happened to her and to the sacrifice too in detail.

While Lojain was out of her consciousness, the creature picked up its victim, who was caught by three men. The victim ran in terror and tried to save her life by escaping into the woods. However, the three men were way faster than she was. They brought her back to the village, placed her over a huge block of stone, and one of the men hit her head with a solid magmatic rock until blood burst out of it. The creature appeared and approached the victim, flipped her on her face and took out his reap hook to cut the victim's body and enjoy the taste of her blood. It chopped off her head, sucked it till drained and then ordered the villagers to hang it up the oak tree.

It chopped her arms along with the backbone and started to enjoy the taste. Later, it ordered the villagers to hang that part up the fig tree. It kept chopping the victim's body and asked for each part to be hanged up a different tree.

Draining the body from blood, the creature asked for the unconscious woman to be brought to his feet and they obeyed. They placed Lojain on the same block of stone. It ordered them to flip Lojain on the face. The gypsies were thrilled thinking that the spell would be broken if a sacrifice was made by a stranger; however, the creature was smarter than the villagers.

It started to move its hand over Lojain's head while mumbling few words by which he made Lojain forget all that happened and all what she had seen before losing consciousness.

After she was flipped over, it undressed her back, took out a small inverted cross and placed it over three different spots of her back for three minutes: the right side, the left side, and her backbone; a minute for each spot. It started to mumble words, that can only be understood by the likes of such creature, so that when she would wake up, she would be scared to death and forget everything about that incident.

End of Part Two

**Part Three
113 Gypsies**

Prologue

It became clear that the creature was after that village in particular. Why? What have they done to it?

Let's dig back in time.

Thirteen years ago, the creature went out with its son to horrify the neighboring villages. The son was 333 years old; a strong hunter of souls and bodies. It used to haunt people down for their blood; however, sometimes it did it for fun. Its father tried to train it well as it was the worthiest of his thirty brothers to carry on the legacy of the family. Those thirty brothers had always tried to play their young brother false.

Note

These creatures go out only on the thirteenth day of each month to hunt people down and have their version of fun.

One day, as these creatures were getting ready for their raids, going after blood and entertainment, all of the them went out except for Hareth, who was the meanest of all.

Hareth planned to deceive his little brother. The night before the raid (i.e. on the twelfth day of the month), he went to the village, which the pack had planned to attack and asked to meet with the chief of the village. Hareth told the chief about the attack planned for the following day to kill everyone in there.

Moreover, Hareth made a plan with the chief; he told the chief that the weakest point of the pack was the youngest part of it which was known for its pink color. Let's not forget to tell you that the young brother had a pink patch on its neck and Wardy[1] was his name.

Hareth left the village after setting the scene for his plan of betrayal. It set up all traps to catch Wardy.

The attack on the gypsies' village commenced in the absence of the twenty-nine brothers as only Wardy and its father were still following the attack plan. The father sensed the deception of its sons and retreated at once; however, the pampered son was still following the plan on his own. Wardy fell a victim to all the traps that were set up for it; it was stabbed, caught, and held in an iron net as another man was stabbing it with a dagger.

The son was killed, the father became the prey of its own sorrows and the son's soul turned into a ghost. But, where should the father start taking revenge? Should it start with the betraying sons or the gypsies?

The father attacked its twenty-nine sons as it soared over the gypsies' village. Wherever it caught one of the sons, it shed its blood over the village while mumbling certain words to cast its eternal spell.

The father's heart perished while it was cutting its twenty-nine sons' bodies into pieces. It went to the village chief and told him about the spell, which would only be broken after

---

[1] Wardy means pinky in Arabic

shedding the blood of its inhabitants. It should visit the village once a month to reap a soul for sacrifice.

End of Part Three

Part Four
Last Part
113 Gypsies

Prologue

A fly's memory is a short-termed one; as the fly forgets whatever it has been through. Why do we not make our lives as well as our bad memories temporary till they just disappear?

Getting back to the present time:

Lojain decided to follow the gypsies and help them get rid of the creature besides its avidity and terror. She dug into old books and manuscripts tackling such creatures and put her mind into it. She searched all the woods in the area till she managed to locate them as they were camping by the side of a fresh water spring, which was overlooked by a breathtaking waterfall. Lojain tried to have a word with the gypsies' chief so that she could advise him on a way to break the spell and get rid of that creature. The gypsies guided her to the chief's dwelling. He was an old man yet he led a whole village!

Lojain found her way into the chief's shelter. He told her about the attack they had years ago and she told him about the solution she had reached to break the spell.

As she was diving into the old manuscripts and books while looking for a solution to break the spell that was once cast on the gypsies, she found out that a solution was to sacrifice a stranger. The chief agreed to that solution and prayed it would pull off.

The thirteenth night of the month came for the creature to appear and claim its new sacrifice and enjoy the taste of its blood!

"Where is my sacrifice, wicked gypsies?!" the creature shouted.

The villagers pointed at the block of stone on which a girl was fastened and secured. It flew toward the sacrifice as fast as lightning and started to cut it into seven parts while sucking each part. Then, it happened!

The villagers danced with joy that the curse was broken; the stranger girl they had sacrificed was Lojain!

When Lojain entered the chief's shelter, she told him that she would sacrifice herself provided that the whole incident would be videotaped. Later, the cameras would be sent to the publishing house, where she worked.

The curse, which had plagued the village for years, was finally broken.

A girl had sacrificed her life to save a whole village.

End of Story

Epilogue

We never know what our next card holds; goodness or evilness!
Let's make it a white one packed with goodness.

Soulmate I

Prologue

We can never know when and where we would meet the right one with whom we shall spend the rest of our lives.

Saleh and Antonila were cousins. Saleh was born to devoted Emirati Muslim parents, who were married traditionally after their families had met.

As for Antonila, she had a French mother and an Emirati father. Antonila was born during her father's scholarship after marrying her Christian mother, Maria.

Antonila took after her mother; she was blonde, slim with blue eyes, and very small lips.

Antonila's father graduated and received his doctorate in psychology after few years of studying abroad.

When it was time to get back home, Meshaal – Antonila's father – booked the flight tickets for his family and he was received by his father at the airport. They hugged tightly as they were overwhelmed with joy for seeing one another. Mishaal's father realized that two people were standing next to his son and asked who they were. Meshaal promised that he would tell him all about it once they got home.

An hour later, they entered the house and Antonila's father started to tell his family the story of meeting his wife.

"But, we are a devoted Muslim family, how could you bring a Christian wife to be our daughter in law?!" his father wondered.

Arguments started to escalate, the family wanted their daughter-in-law to convert to Islam or else their son would have to divorce her. Meshaal wanted to calm the situation by taking more time to convince Maria to convert to Islam.

During such phase of convincing, Maria wanted to know more about Islam before converting to it as for the last nine years she had spent with Meshaal in France, she knew nothing about it and Meshaal did not talk that much about his religious background.

Nevertheless, Maria was never convinced by converting from Christianity to Islam just to please her husband's father. She refused the suggestion of the convincing phase. She simply wanted to remain a Christian wife.

She informed Meshaal of her decision.

What should I do now, what should I tell my father, Meshaal wondered.

Meshaal tried to put some pressure on Maria, but her opinion never changed.

After a While...

Meshaal had a new job in one of Abu Dhabi's most remarkable hospitals with a considerable salary. Maria was thrilled to hear such news and she told her husband that she wanted to leave his father's house as soon as possible. Meshaal was opposed to the idea, claiming that he owned half of it. Maria was left in tears; her dream of having her own house was ruined.

At the same time, Antonila was introduced to the family members including her uncle's family. All she could see among them was the only one her heart leaped for.

They fell in love despite their young age; Saleh was now only sixteen and Antonila was two years younger than him. They started to learn each other's languages. Antonila became Saleh's French teacher and he became her Arabic one.

During the time they started to know one another, Antonila became fluent in Arabic and Saleh too became a fluent French speaker; however, no one could tell that it was also the time when their love sparked.

Wherever the family members would gather, Saleh and Antonila would stay near each other. They would take those long walks by the sea, roast steak at home, and learn more. When they were at home, they made sure not to cause any suspicion so that no one would know about their love story.

Suddenly and Out of Nowhere...

Maria woke up one day, packed her bags to leave her husband, and get back to her country. She even told Meshaal that he should either travel back to France with her or divorce her so she could leave with her daughter.

Meshaal's father was glad to hear that and asked his son to pick the divorce option; after all, Maria was not a Muslim.

Meshaal was at his wits end; if he agreed to divorce his wife, she would take Antonila away and he could not imagine life in her absence.

As Things Escalated...

Antonila saw it all! She shed so many tears while wondering why this was happening. She had to leave her love, the man who was a source of security for her. Saleh was confused and was not sure what to do; he was too young to fight the elders of the family over it!

End of Part One

Soulmate II

Prologue

Man's will prevails all! If a man wants to achieve something, he has to go for it.

Meshaal wanted to fix things with his wife but the gap started to widen between the married couple.

Maria packed her bags as well as Antonila's and got ready to head to the French embassy.

Antonila was crying her heart out as she had to leave the man she loved, the man for whom she learned Arabic and from whom she learned about Islam – her cousin, Saleh!

Antonila left and took Saleh's heart with her. Maria called a cab to take them to the embassy and on the way, she told Meshaal that she wanted a divorce, urging him to send her the divorce papers as soon as he could so that she could carry on with her life in France.

Antonila was supposed to stay with her father; however, her French citizenship prevented her from doing so. Actually, the embassy refused too.

The tickets were booked and Saleh's heart was packed in Antonila's bags. Maria made it to Nice in the company of her daughter where Maria started looking for a job and managed to find two. She worked as a bartender at night and a waitress during the day.

Antonila joined the university, where she chose her father's major; Psychology. She was hardworking and excelled at each course she had taken.

Four Years Later...

Antonila turned into a young lady at her twenty-fourth birthday. She graduated with a diploma in medicine and wanted to carry on with her studies to gain a higher degree in the same field.

One Night...

Antonila joined her mother at a concert, where they could have a chance to dance to the music. Suddenly and unexpectedly, everything around them changed, as a terrorist stole a big van and drove it in a crowded street, causing a lot of deaths among foreigners and locals.

At the same time, Antonila's cries of pain could be heard; the terrorist driver hit her and injured her leg badly. However, those cries turned out to be rather over her mother's dead body lying before her eyes.

Antonila was drowned in sorrow and tears. When the time had come to bury the victims of such incident including Maria, Antonila wore black and lighted candles to commemorate the memory of her mother.

What should I do now?! she wondered. *Without having my mother around, this country is now a strange place for me.*

Back in the Emirates...

Saleh had just graduated from the university with a BA in Architecture Engineering. Immediately, he started to receive job offers to establish buildings in Dubai and Abu Dhabi.

Eng. Saleh started to establish his own business in engineering. He became a man of wealth at the age of twenty-six; however, the memory of that girl he once had loved never left him.

Saleh's father – Khalifa – passed away two years before his graduation, but that had never affected his life nor his academic performance. Actually, Salah hated his father as the latter was the one always urging his grandfather to force Meshaal to divorce Maria; in other words, Khalifa was the one that parted Saleh and Antonila.

End of Part Two

Would it happen?! Would Saleh and Antonila meet again?

Soulmate III

Prologue

A man seeking success shall know the taste of it after a journey of planning for his own future.

Realizing all the successes he had made in building remarkable and massive companies, Saleh's company itself became one of the biggest construction companies in the Emirates; however, something was always missing in his life i.e., having someone to share such successes with.

Saleh tried hard to get Antonila's address in France through her embassy in the UAE, but he always received "NO" as an answer. The embassy argued that Saleh's reasons for such request were not convincing.

Saleh explained that Antonila was his cousin and that he wanted to know what had become of her. The embassy did not respond to his request, so he decided to use his money to get such data. Indeed, he managed to get the data he sought; money could play a major part to help those in need. He received the following data:

Name: Antonila Maria Gasquet
Address: Nice
Apartment: 13, Promenade des Anglais.

Such data were valuable for Saleh to find his cousin living in France.

Graduating from Nice University with a degree in Psychology, Antonila had a job in the French capital city, Paris, in Hotel Dieu Hospital, allegedly established back in 651AD to make the oldest hospital in Paris.

That was fate! Once Saleh had managed to get her address in Nice, Antonila moved to another city, namely Paris.

Saleh traveled to Nice once he had the chance to. He booked flight tickets and arranged for his accommodation. He started to arrange his schedule while being in that city so that he could look for his love and take care of his business at the same time.

The air was clear and the flight did not take more time than the expected i.e., 5:55 hrs. Saleh left the plane filled with hope that he would finally meet with his cousin, Antonila.

He rested for the first day. On the following day, he called some engineers and asked to meet with them to go through their plans in Nice.

The engineers were taken by his fluency as he did not employ a translator to help him during the meeting. He also kept in touch with them to know what they needed and what he needed too.

The Meeting Was Over...

Saleh joined his driver and headed to the address he had received from the embassy. At each and every red light, his heart kept leaping. Finally, he was about to meet the girl he had been parted with for long years.

The car reached the street. Saleh asked about the building and headed to the apartment; however, he was shocked to hear that she had left it!

After knowing the story behind his visit and after trusting him, the woman living next door told him that Antonila had got a job in the capital city hospital and handed him an address.

Immediately, Saleh headed to the airport to fly to Paris. Two hours and 971 kms later, he reached his destination.

He headed to the hospital at once and booked a session with his cousin as a regular patient to surprise her. He used his driver's name to book the session.

Numbers kept changing as he was waiting for his own number to come up. It did!

He entered into the examination room and talked to her in French so that she would not suspect it.

"What is wrong, Mr. Andrea?" she inquired.

He told her that at the age of eighteen he fell in love with that girl, who taught him everything about love and French and that he also taught her everything about Islam and Arabic.

As Saleh or Andrea was telling Antonila what had been wrong with him, she raised her head to see the man she had lost years ago. Memories started to flow back.

"Yes, dear cousin! It's me, Saleh! Your cousin," he replied as he was getting down on his knees holding a diamond ring.

She agreed immediately, hugged him without hesitation, and they kissed.

Saleh moved to the French city and married Antonila; a Christian wife and a Muslim husband living in peace and well-being.

End of Story

Seek love till you find it!

Note:

All the names of the cities, streets, terrorist attacks, and places are real. Moreover, the timing of the plane flight is real too, but the story is imaginary.

The Last Trip

Prologue

Once, a friend said,

"Do not wait for people to do anything for you. If you want to build something, build it yourself. If you want to bring it down, do it yourself. Be yourself because you always shine."

Nourah graduated from high school with a degree with distinction as she scored 99.9% in addition to 99.3 in general abilities exam which was the score that would let one into a prestigious university for any major one could think of.

However, Nourah wanted to complete her studies abroad and her choice was approved by her father and family. Her file was uploaded and supported by a governmental document usually issued by the ministry to get a scholarship abroad.

Months later, Nourah did not receive any news regarding the scholarship. Hence, her father decided to head to the ministry with his daughter to meet with the minister, who signed the papers.

Nourah's father did not have much connections, but the scores his daughter had achieved were the reason why she was granted the scholarship.

Procedures were finalized, the ticket was booked, and the Visa was issued under the category of "student Visa." The interview at the New Zealander embassy was done and the Visa was approved.

On the day Nourah was ready to travel, she saw off her mother and siblings with tears as if they were saying goodbye to a dying person. At the airport, it was time to say goodbye to her father, whom she was going to leave for seven years. She burst into tears. Her flight number was called and she hurried to catch it.

The officer gave the last approval of her acceptance to leave the country.

On the Plane...

Nourah was terrified! A flight attendant tried to calm her down. She took Nourah's ticket, showed her to her seat, and handed her a pillow to rest. The plane took off.

It was lunch time. They brought her lunch, but she barely touched it; she was already missing her mother. Halfway there, suddenly, the plane shook severely as the right engine exploded, followed by the second.

Calls and screams started to fill the cabin. The pressure inside the cabin kept growing till the doors were broken open and passengers started to fly out of the plane. Nourah and the flight attendant were holding one another tightly, but that did not last for long; the air pressure was so high that it pulled away the flight attendant, whose body was shredded in the burning engine. As for Nourah, she gave up! She unfastened her seatbelt and was pulled out of the cabin.

She hit her face on the wing and bled. She could not feel a thing because she had given up and admitted defeat to death!

While she was floating in the air, she recalled her mother, father, and siblings. She remembered all the memories she had shared with them. Surely, they would miss her!

She reached the land and hit her head hard.

Well, Nourah fell off her bed and her head hit the ground because she was asleep, having a nightmare.

"Thank God it was a nightmare!" she said.

A Tip:

All our dreams can come true only if we do not lose hope.

November 1st

Prologue

Be a good model for those who look up to you!

In a humid night of the Eastern Province of the Kingdom of Saudi Arabia – namely Al Khubar – Anas was running next to the sea side to relieve some of the work stress. To lose that headache, he would either spend that time running or drinking his afternoon coffee at the Dhahran Mall.

He was sitting at one of the single tables sipping his coffee while going through his mobile applications such as Twitter and WhatsApp.

Anas was bored and kept thinking about ways to enjoy his time. He thought about calling his friends, but they were all busy and not picking up the phone would increase his boredom.

Suddenly, a white girl sat next to him. She had a mole under her right eye, her hands were adorned with henna, and her perfume was out of this world!

"Yes, sister! How can I help you?" Anas asked.

"Do not be afraid! I came with good news for you," softly, she replied.

"What good news would make a girl that I do not know sit next to me sharing my table?!" Anas wondered.

The girl told Anas that she wanted to marry him and asked for his phone number. Anas laughed loudly till he attracted the attention of those around and then asked her to leave the table.

"I will not leave till you give me what I have asked for," she said.

Anas was shocked and confused. Her eyes were burning with seriousness, he could feel it. He kept quiet for a second...hesitated once, but pulled himself together, and passed her what she had asked for.

It was Monday night, November 1st, when Anas received a call from an unregistered number. Usually, Anas would not pick up if the number was unregistered; however, he had already installed a program to reveal the caller's name.

It read the name Mashaael Abdullah. Anas picked it up and their conversation started and lasted for long times. Mashaael started to tell Anas about her personal life, but he never shared his.

Anas recalled the fact that he was a married man with children and told Mashaael, who could not care less. Her target was Anas and no one else!

She told Anas that she was the daughter of a well-known family. She also told him that she was well-heeled and that her father was a consultant physician working for one of Dammam's remarkable bodies.

Anas could not care less about her wealth or anything else except for two things; the kid living with her and the reason why she was after him!

He shared with her his thoughts.

"He is my son from a previous marriage," she explained.

Mashaael told Anas about her previous husband who used to drink and abuse her till she got a divorce. As for the second part of the inquiry, she wanted to marry Anas.

End of Part One

Part Two

Will Anas and Mashaael get married?
Trust should be mutual, otherwise things will turn out badly!

Part Two
November 1st

Prologue

Man may sacrifice to achieve the happiness of others.

Anas rented a small room in Dammam so that he would be free to contact Mashaael whenever she called. He left his apartment in Al Khubar waiting for her call and dying to know what would happen next.

At one o'clock at noon and after finishing his work, Anas received a call from Mashaael.

"Hi, Anas! How are you doing? You must be tired after work! What about grabbing lunch somewhere?" she suggested.

Anas agreed at once; just to know what would happen next.

She sent him the address to an amazing restaurant that looked over the sea.

At two o'clock, he arrived at the restaurant to find that everything had been set up. He was amazed and thought about how he would pay for all this!

Suddenly, a man entered along with Mashaael and her young boy to join Anas' table.

"This is Abdullah Saleh, my father," Mashaael introduced the man in her company.

Anas introduced himself too while feeling amazed and embarrassed by the situation.

They started chatting and Anas forgot about the reason why he had come to that place. He also forgot about how tiresome he had been feeling earlier as Abdullah's tête-à-tête seemed open and interesting.

They had a long conversation till it was time for the father to leave the scene and his daughter remained in Anas' company.

"Why did you do that?" Anas asked.

Mashaael wanted to make it clear for Anas that she had an open-minded father, but it seemed that Anas was not in favor of such fact, so he intended to leave the restaurant. He asked for the cheque to pay for the lunch, but it turned out that Mashaael had that covered.

What was going on? Anas, as a "man" felt a bit offended; how could a woman pay for their lunch?!

At a heavenly scene as the sun was going down, they took long walks by Dammam corniche.

Sometimes, he shared his thoughts with her and she revealed a secret of hers too. Once, she told him that her beauty was fake. She explained that she had an accident that disfigured her face as well as a big part of her chest. She had the plastic surgeries she needed done. She told Anas about everything that she had gone through and he was a good listener. Sometimes, he felt sorry for her and other times, he could not stop those feelings of abhorrence he experienced. At that night, he made up his mind and decided to know what would happen next with Mashaael. A girl of her wealth wanted to marry an already married man!

At eleven o'clock, under the moonlight, Anas started to talk to her openly. "You are a beautiful woman, Mashaael! But, I'm a married man, I can never be in a relationship with another woman," he explained.

She told him that she still wanted to be with him even if it was in secrecy. She could not leave him, but he did not want to have it that way. He had to choose to stay either with his wife, with whom he had spent so many years of his life, or with Mashaael.

They could not reach a way out of such dilemma. Would Anas marry her? Till the moment that story was written!

End of Part Two

Would there be another part of the story? We do not know!

(Based on a true story.)

Part One
A False Promise

Prologue

Always, trust your capabilities to satisfy yourself, not others!

People make promises every day. Some of them fulfill such promises, others forget all about them while few others even deny making any.

They were three girls, who made a promise to stay friends for life. They were all of the same age: twenty-three, but they were different in height, color, and religion.

Their families knew nothing about such friendship otherwise they would try to separate them.

Sarah: The white, beautiful Jew, who was just towards everyone. Her father owned a jewelry store.

Maria: The poor Christian girl living on the crumbs of others. She was white, but her face was disfigured due to an accident she had. When she was a kid, the house of her foster family burned down leaving her with a scar on half of her face.

Zainab: The Muslim girl. She was dark-skinned, veiled, devoted, and pure. She always wore black. Her father was a descendant of religious scholars. He was rich and owned a real estate office.

The three girls met during the second year of their university as they shared the same major; Psychology. They met and immediately became best friends. They never asked themselves about their religions or social statuses.

They exchanged numbers. In the evening, Zainab called both Maria and Sarah to go out. They picked out a restaurant near to Zainab's house and showed up in no time. Zainab booked a room to dine in.

Zainab ordered a huge amount of vegetables as she was a vegetarian and topped it with an orange juice. Sarah ordered kosher meat (any type of meat that is free of fats and grease- milk and meat must not be mixed in Judaism) along with grape juice. As for Maria, she never said "No" to food, whatever it was.

As they talked, Zainab told the girls that she would make an oath of blood with them to not be parted ever. Immediately, Sarah and Maria picked up their knives and cut their hands. They placed their hands on one another's and promised not to be parted no matter what.

Dinner was over and they left the restaurant, heading to Zainab's house that was nearby. Zainab invited them to meet with her family.

At the house, Zainab's parents showed up and sat next to the girls. Zainab's father was disturbed to see a cross hanging over Maria's neck as well as a star of David hanging over Sarah's. He winked at his daughter to follow him as Zainab's mother was left to chat with the girls.

In the Room

Zainab had a heated argument with her father.

"Are you aware what religious backgrounds they have?" the father asked.

"No, I do not know! But, when we met, we did not care that much about it," Zainab replied.

"You shall not be friends with those girls any more or else I will be angry with you," he threatened.

Zainab was perplexed; should she disobey her father or should she part with her friends, who were extremely confused about Zainab's attitude; how could she invite them to her house and kick them out this way? What about the oath they had made not so long ago!

"Get out of my father's house at once!" Zainab tried to wink at the girls as she screamed.

The girls got it and left the place.

That night, the girls left Zainab's house with so many questions running all over in their heads.

Back to Zainab's house, the father started to scold his daughter to make sure that she would not talk to them ever again. Zainab obeyed her father and picked up the phone to call the girls and ask them not to talk to her ever again. She also told them that her father was hearing the phone call as well.

The Next Morning...

Zainab's father took her to the university and reminded her of last night. Zainab lowered her head as if she had agreed to his words.

As she got in, she could see the girls to whom she winked. Then, she looked back at her father and waved.

Zainab headed to the cafe, where she met with the other two girls. She told them about last night's scolding. The three girls promised to keep their friendship a secret.

End of Part One

Part Two
A False Promise

Prologue

We make our own decisions willingly, but when it comes to tell who we will fall in love with, we have nothing to say but to follow our hearts and minds.

It was Saturday noon when they called for Dhuhr prayer. The city was filled with sounds coming from mosques and temples as each girl headed her own way to perform her prayer. Later, they met again, greeted one another, cared for nothing, and got into the university together. Maria greeted her group of friends, who were mainly males except for Sarah and Zainab, who were a bit surprised by such a thing. What did they want from Maria?

They called Maria at once and Zainab started to yell at Maria.

"What do these boys want from you?!" Zainab asked.

Maria told them that she worked at night in a brothel to pay for her university fees! Zainab and Sarah's hearts broke into a million pieces. *Have we got that low?!*

The girls did not give Maria any piece of advice, they felt sorry for her but there was nothing they could do!

At Midnight...

Maria headed to the brothel as Sarah was following her from a distance to get its location and report it to the police before Maria got in. But, Maria was there before time. At two o'clock after midnight, a bushed Maria came out of the brothel heading to her foster family's house.

In the University...

The girls met in the plaza. Maria was extremely exhausted. Sarah told Zainab about the place Maria had been to and together they planned to call the police to arrest the brothel companions...

Sarah called the police and made a plan to meet them at a certain point at midnight. A couple of police cars came as planned along with Sarah and Zainab, who immediately got hold of Maria before she entered the suspected house. Later, the police burst into the brothel and arrested everyone inside.

"Let go of me! Let me get in! I have no money to pay for my university fees," Maria yelled.

"Calm down, Maria! We have a solution for this. Do not worry about it!" Zainab assured her as she calmed down.

The police officer said that he wanted Maria to be a witness against those criminals and for that she would be rewarded. Moreover, Zainab and Sara would also be rewarded. Furthermore, the girls agreed to give their own reward to Maria. As a turn of tides, the Christian officer caught sight of the cross hanging over Maria's neck and fell in love with her. Maria's name was not included within the suspected list; she was rather one of the witnesses.

She was interrogated and briefed. Later, they called her foster father to come and pick her up. When he arrived at the police station, he was received by the officer, who congratulated him for having such a daughter like Maria.

"You have a brave daughter and she was rewarded for that," the officer said while shaking Maria's foster father's hand and asked for their home address.

The Following Day...

The officer arrived at Maria's foster family's house to ask for her hand in marriage. George, Maria's foster father, was thrilled and agreed. Maria was over the moon as now things would become easier to handle…

End of Part Two

Part Three
A False Promise

Prologue

Having faith in God's plan and arrangements.

Maria was engaged to the police officer, Fady, who suggested to have their marriage concluded two months later. Maria was happy and agreed to everything Fady had suggested.

Her friends; Sarah and Zainab, showed up at the engagement party.

George did not complain about the presence of a Jew or a Muslim in his house, especially before the police officer; however, when the party was done and after Sarah and Zainab had left along with Fady's family, George started to scold Maria.

"If you do not stop seeing those girls, I will not let you marry Fady," he threatened.

Maria could not utter a single word, she simply nodded!

At the University...

Maria told her friends about the last night's confrontation she had had with her foster father, whose situation seemed confusing for Sarah and Zainab. They thought that he had been very kind to them at the engagement party as he kept serving them everything on the menu! Maria told them that he was that kind because he did not wish to make a scene in the presence of her fiancé. He wanted the night to end without any damage.

Maria told them that it would not be possible for them to attend the wedding ceremony; however, she promised to hold them a party of their own.

Lectures ended and each girl headed home except for Sarah, who joined her father at his jewelry to help him. Sarah's father was a fanatic to the extent that he refused to sell his goods to non-Jews.

Maria and Fady decided to go out and buy things for their marriage and new home. They saw a jewelry store and went inside. Once Sarah saw Maria and her fiancé, she welcomed them to her father's shop.

Sarah's father was delighted with the way his daughter had treated her clients.

"So, tell me what brought you here?" Sarah asked.

"We just wanted to get a diamond ring for the engagement," Maria replied.

"Well, let's see what we have in here!" Sarah said as she pulled out a wide set of rings.

"No! I will get them something from our special hidden collection." Sarah's father stepped in.

Sarah was thrilled that her father was very considerate while dealing with her good friend and her fiancé. He brought out an album and sat next to the couple. Suddenly, his eyes widened with surprise as he saw the cross hanging over Maria's neck. His face expressions changed as well as his attitude.

"I have no gold or jewelry to sell here. Get out of here right now!" he ordered.

Fady was frustrated and started to attack Sarah's father verbally.

"I sell only to those I desire. This is my shop. Get out now!" Isaac, Sarah's father, said.

After Fady had left the shop with his fiancée, he started to scold Maria and told her not to meet Sarah ever again.

Back at the store, Sarah's cries of pain were heard as Isaac was violently beating her until she bled. At that point, Isaac called for an ambulance to save Sarah's life. The paramedics showed up and took Sarah to the hospital, where they were told that an investigation would be conducted. However, Sarah said that she was not beaten and that she fell off her father's building.

Investigators questioned Sarah's father, who gave the exact statement. He claimed that his daughter had fallen off the building and that he had witnesses of the incident.

Later, Isaac went into his daughter's room to thank her as she did not tell the investigator about the confrontation they had in the shop.

Sarah asked to keep her friendship with Maria, but her father refused such condition and made it clear that he would rather have her killed or dead before she made friends with non-Jews. Sarah was at a loss! She did not know what to do. Eventually, she decided to tell the girls about it and keep their friendship a secret.

At the University...

There was a heart that always leaped for seeing Zainab; it was Sameh's – the Christian student, who made up his mind and went to talk to her. Her appearance made him realize that she was a Muslim.

Their relationship started to grow stronger by the day. Zainab was not aware of Sameh's religious background, but her love was bigger than that. Sameh decided to propose to Zainab and asked for her home address.

"What would you need my home address for?" she wondered.

"I want to propose to you!" Sameh replied.

Zainab blushed and lowered her head as if she was just saying "Yes, I do!" She gave him the address.

Maria and Sarah hurried to congratulate Zainab, who was terrified as if her heart knew how Sameh's encounter with her father would be like.

Sameh followed the address to Zainab's house and knocked on the door, which was answered by her young brother.

"Is your father home?" Sameh asked.

"Yes, he is!" the kid answered as a man appeared at the door.

He had a long beard and was a frightening sight, at least to Sameh.

"Please, come in!" Zainab's father offered.

"Oh! No, thank you! It seems that I got the wrong address." Sameh declined the offer.

Sameh ran away after seeing Zainab's father.

The Next Day...

Sameh told Zainab that he was a Christian.

"I had never thought that you are! I have many Christian friends, but none of them is a coward like you. Now, I get it. I do not care anymore. Just go away and leave me!" Zainab commented.

Each night, Zainab cried her heart out and each night, Sarah and Maria came over to ease her pains.

End of Part Three

Part Four

Last Part

A False Promise

Prologue

A man's journey may be long and tiring, but he shall reach his destination after all.

After all the agony, pains, and tiredness the girls had been through, they decided to keep their friendship a secret to save themselves the confrontations they had with their fathers.

The fourth term was about to wrap up and the university decided to arrange a trip for its Psychology Department for recreation. The university sent papers with each student to be signed by their parents as the trip would last for a whole week.

Maria and Sarah had to lie to their fathers as the girls told them that they needed to go on that trip in order to finish their courses successfully.

Immediately, both fathers agreed. On the other hand, Zainab told her father the truth that the university had decided to arrange for that trip for recreation and that parents' approval was required. Unexpectedly, her father agreed and handed her a large amount of money to spend there after she promised him that she would adhere to her hijab and prayers. Zainab was thrilled for her father's trust in her.

On the Day of the Trip...

Each student brought the approval slip of their parents in addition to the fees and handed them to the organizers.

Inside the Bus...

Each girl was seated next to a guy except for the three girls, who wanted to sit together.

Songs and joy started to fill the air inside the bus as students kicked off the trip.

The bus driver stopped for gas and some students left the bus to get things from the station market. When the driver decided to stop, he had planned to sip some alcohol without getting caught, so he headed to an isolated spot, got his bottle out, and started to drink. The students went back to the bus, so did the drunk driver, who seemed unconscious while being behind the wheel. He moved from the left lane to the right one facing the cars coming the opposite side of the road. The bus got into an accident and left behind thirteen deaths, including himself. Seven girls and six guys were dead including the three secret friends.

News was aired on the death of a group of students on the coastal road. The names were announced as parents were sitting in homes waiting. The anchor announced the names of Maria George, Zainab Abdullah, and Sarah Isaac. Each family drowned in tears and agony for their losses. During each girl's funeral, fathers would meet to console one another; the Christian and the Jewish fathers would show up at the Muslim's funeral, the Muslim and the Christian fathers would show up at the Jew's funeral, the Muslim and the Jewish fathers would show up at the Christian's funeral. Each had its own funeral held in the church, the temple, and the mosque. Black was the color they all shared.

End of Story

The Hypocrite Sister-in-Law

Prologue

Hypocrisy comes in all shades...

After a long and tiring day at work, Saber entered his father, Ayoub's house with a piece of news that he wanted to share with the whole family. He told them that he had made up his mind to marry a girl, who had lost both her parents.

Some of the family members were thrilled to hear such news while others opposed to it as Saber was already a married man!

Saber forgot about it; he thought of his wife and what would happen to her if he did it!

At the same time, one of Saber' sisters-in-law overheard the discussions he had with his brothers.

A while later, the sister-in-law did not come along with her husband to his father's house; however, she headed to her sister's and spread some fake news contrary to what had happened. It was Saber who was going to get married, but the sister-in-law's envy and hatred made her claim that Hany was the one getting married to that girl!

Then, the sister of that sister-in-law headed to Hany's uncle house (his father-in-law) and called Hany's wife to confirm the news, whether it was true or not!

Troubles between Hany and his wife intensified because of a single lie. Immediately, Hany went to his uncle's house (his wife's father) and found out who was the reason behind conveying such false news. The problem was solved, but the apathy between Hany and his wife still remained; because of the hypocrite sister-in-law.

Moral:

Keep quiet in times that you may lose a brother, a sister, a mother, or a father.

End of Story

Part One
Mannar

A mirror may reflect the truth lying before it; however, it can never reflect what is buried in the heart of man.

Souad was the wife of a businessman, who was always on the road. He was a rich and a smart man, who invested all his time in order to make money and fall in love with the world. They were not love birds before they got married, but time stepped in and attached them to one another. Moreover, Wagdy had always wanted to have a son to whom he would leave his inheritance.

Souad was not happy with that marriage, but her parents were blinded by their love for money and that was the reason they gave their daughter away in marriage to Wagdy.

Two Months Later...

Wagdy received a heartwarming piece of news when he learned that his wife, Souad, was pregnant! Out of his heartfelt happiness, he made a cheque of $130000 for his wife as well as another one of $30000 for the baby.

He was not yet familiar with the baby's sex and being overwhelmed with such joy, Wagdy hired every servant he could get in order to make life easier for his wife.

Days turned into months and months passed by as Souad's due date approached. Her husband stayed at her side, leaving behind his business, and waited to see who would be the one to inherit his legacy. Was it a boy? Or was it a girl?

At midnight, Souad went into labor and she started screaming to announce the coming of the baby. Immediately, Wagdy took his wife to the nearest hospital.

At the hospital, the nurses and doctors, whom Wagdy had hired to deliver his baby and bring him happiness, were running up and down the corridors.

"Congratulations! You have a beautiful baby girl…white-skinned, normal weight, and steady pulse." the doctor brought in the good news.

No words could describe Wagdy's happiness. He was overwhelmed and he started to give away dollars to everyone around. He almost forgot about his wife. Actually, he did not inquire about her medical condition.

The doctor got Souad and her baby out of the delivery room for the father to see them. Wagdy was on the top of the world. He told Souad that he would give the baby girl the name "Mannar"[2] so that she would lighten his path in life with joy and happiness. Souad did not show any opposition to Wagdy's decision. Actually, she was not conscious due to her pains.

A Week Later…

Souad and the baby were dismissed from the hospital and Wagdy had already prepared for their homecoming; he had a

---

[2] Mannar is a name derived from light in Arabic.

place equipped to suit his baby girl and hired two nannies for her.

Mannar kept growing up before the eyes of her mother. As for the father, he went back to his busy schedule, traveling from one country to another in order to collect money.

On a Very Bad Day...

A violent storm blew, leading to the suspension of all flights; however, the money seeker was blinded by his passion and rented a car to transport him.

On the road, the rain shower kept pouring in a way that blocked the sight of the driver, who had to pull over.

"Keep driving and I will double the fare," Wagdy promised.

The driver carried on his way as the rain shower got heavier. The storm got stronger that it started to pull off trees and move blocks of stones all over the way. The driver wanted to stop again, but Wagdy made him carry on the trip by promising him to double the fare again!

A moment later, a huge tree carried by the storm hit the car severely and crushed it into pieces.

The next day, as the storm calmed down, the police came to look for any missing persons. They found the car that had been smashed by the storm. They also found two unidentified human bodies.

The police called for the ambulance to come and pick the two bodies and to deliver them to the forensic lab for identification.

Back at the site of the accident, the police kept looking for any identity documents for either of the bodies and they managed to find the driver's only. As for the second passenger, their papers had been scattered by the strong storm. In the forensic lab, they managed to identify the other body; it was the body of Wagdy. His death was broadcasted in the news.

Back in the house, Souad and Mannar were playing in the garden where the maids came in with the news. Souad lost her consciousness. As for Mannar, she was too young to understand what was going on around.

After a while, Souad came back to her senses. She started to cry over her dead husband. She started also to wear black in grief. Her family came to console her. The mourning period ended, but still Souad was in black. Her father told her that the mourning period should only last for three days. She obeyed her father and changed her colors.

The next day, the lawyer visited Souad to tell her that all Wagdy's fortune had been registered under his daughter's name, leaving Souad the shares of the European company.

Immediately, Souad sold all her shares in that company so that she could live with her daughter and raise her up.

One year followed another, Mannar grew up and reached the legal age. She started to invest the money she inherited from her father well by purchasing a group of low-cost buildings, demolishing them and rebuilding them again to be in a better condition. Her mother could only see Wagdy in her daughter's image; Mannar was seeking money like her father once did.

End of Part One

Part Two
Mannar

Prologue

When we miss paradise, we could see mothers.

Souad's father, Abdullah, wanted his daughter to get married after the years she had spent raising her daughter. Whenever he broached the subject, she opposed, claiming that she had to be there for her daughter. Now, as her daughter was a grown up, would not it be time for Souad to pay some attention to herself?!

Ramzy was a well-off man. He was tall with gray hair and characteristics similar to those of her late husband. He also travelled a lot for work. He met with Souad to get the chance to know one another. Ramzy's wife had died suffering from cancer and he was in need of a wife too.

They met over dinner and talked for a while. Each was inquiring about the character of the other before getting into talking about marriage.

Mannar came down to meet her future stepfather. She checked him thoroughly, detected the gray hair on his head and fell in love with them as it reminded her of her father's. She agreed on the marriage as if it was her call.

Souad agreed to marry Ramzy because of her daughter. The wedding ceremony was held in her mansion, were she arranged everything.

On the wedding night, Ramzy came with all his family members to celebrate the wedding. Mannar approached her stepfather and started to take pictures with him while holding his right hand as if she was the bride, not her mother. She started to introduce him to her friends, who kept winking at her saying that Ramzy was eye-catching. Mannar simply laughed.

The wedding was over and everyone went home. Concluding the marriage, Ramzy and Souad had one condition that Ramzy would live with Souad in her mansion as she had refused to leave it.

The next day, Ramzy had a considerable commercial deal to make. He had to take his car to finish it. When Souad woke up, she could not find him, so she called him. He told her that he was on a business trip. This brought all the memories back; she recalled everything she had gone through with Wagdy.

Ramzy concluded half the deal and called his wife so that she could prepare his bags as he had to travel to Paris to finalize it. As Souad was preparing her husband's bags in tears, Mannar entered and saw her crying. She asked her mother what was wrong and Souad told her about Ramzy's sudden business trip.

"Why do not you join him? It will be like your honeymoon," Mannar suggested.

"But he did not ask me to prepare mine!" Souad replied.

Mannar picked up the phone and called her stepfather asking him to take her mother on that trip. Ramzy said that it would just take him few hours to sign the deal and get back and that he did not want to be delayed.

Mannar told her mother that he would be in Paris for a couple of hours to get the deal signed and that he would come back to plan on their honeymoon.

Souad's tears were gone as she started to laugh. Moreover, Mannar told her mother that she would travel with Ramzy to gain experience in the field of trade and commerce.

End of Part Two

Part Three
Mannar

Prologue

Mannar travelled to Paris to meet her stepfather, Ramzy. Once she laid her eyes on him, she could see those gray hair and went crazy about it.

"Why don't we eat tonight at one of the French restaurants?" Mannar suggested.

Ramzy agreed after checking his schedule and making sure he was free at that night.

Mannar also booked them a table at one of the fanciest restaurants. She called the reception desk of the hotel and asked them to arrange her and Ramzy a fancy car to take them to the restaurant.

Arriving at the restaurant, they ordered their food. As they were talking over dinner, Mannar told her stepfather that she was in love with him.

Ramzy stopped eating, looked her in the eyes, and he could sense seriousness in her talk.

"I'm your stepfather. You may not say such things to me," Ramzy commented.

"But you remind me of my love for my father. You have to leave my mother and marry me," she suggested.

He yelled at her face and told her to shut up. Everyone around stared at them.

"We need to go now!" he ordered her.

He burst out of the restaurant and headed to the airport directly. He booked two tickets and stayed in silence till they made it back to their country safe and sound. He called her mother, who had been waiting to hear what he had to say.

"We are at a dead end. I have no justification to what I'm saying, but tomorrow I will send you the divorce papers. Please forgive me!" he said.

Ramzy hung up and dropped Mannar at her mansion advising her to love those of her age. She looked at him with a grudge, but he never looked back. He asked the driver to move at once. She kept looking at him till the car disappeared. Entering the mansion, she found her mother soaked in her own blood after she had cut the veins of her hand.

She did not know what to do! She called the police, the ambulance, and then she called her stepfather, who did not pick up. She sent him a message saying that her mother had committed suicide and died. She also asked him to forgive her and told him that she loved him.

First, Mannar buried her father, then she buried her mother too. She wore black and never took it off. She started to recall the memories of her strict father, who kept running after money and business. Eventually, she became an exact copy of him.

End of Story

Najat

Prologue

"Hypocrites in my life are just like paper tissues, you pull one to find another."

Anonymous

Man is created to worship God and to achieve self-existence. Hence, he seeks to provide and secure a respectable life for his children.

Her name was Najat; a beautiful girl born into a well-known and a respectable family. She had an impressive brain with a business vision. Her father owned many companies in a European country. After a while, her father passed away due to his old age, leaving Najat his money as well as the shares in all the companies.

She wanted to liquidate the small companies as well as the low-profit big ones, leaving only two companies to make up her main business.

Najat made it and pulled herself together. She left her sorrows behind and started to look forward to her future. She wanted to be a strong figure in a business community dominated by males.

Hatem was her father's man. He tried to get closer to her in order to become her first assistant, but Najat never trusted men! Months later, he kept trying and with each time he failed to achieve his goal, he tried to convince her that her father used to rely primarily on him. Najat gave it a thought; she inquired about him and with his next attempt, she accepted him to be her assistant.

Later, Najat fell in deep love with Hatem. Despite his poverty, Hatem was never after her money. He proposed to Najat, who agreed at once without even asking for a dowry.

During the time they lived together, she became quite sure of his noble manners. They lived together for a long time and had twin children; a boy and a girl.

One Day...

As Najat was sleeping next to Hatem, she woke up screaming in pain.

"Save me! My brain is going to explode! Help me, my husband," she screamed.

He passed her a pain killer and called the ambulance. They came to pick her up and he joined her ride to the hospital with tearful eyes.

Examinations and procedures started. MRI scans were taken and doctors felt confused. Blood tests were also done. The diagnosis showed that Najat had a brain tumor that had spread. An operation was desperately needed to be performed straightaway.

Hatem was in a tight corner; should he agree to perform the procedure or should they leave Najat to be the victim of her disease? Eventually, as pain was already killing Najat, Hatem agreed to perform the operation with a hope that she could make it.

However, she could not! There was no chance for her; the tumor had spread all over her brain. Najat died and Hatem could only cry in pain. He hugged her tightly.

"Why did you leave me alone like an orphan child?" Hatem mumbled.

He wore black and descended her into her grave. He buried Najat and went back home to cry his heart out.

The following day, the lawyer came to the house and showed Hatem the will Najat had left. She had registered all her money and shares under his name as well as the children's. The girl's name was also Najat;[3] as if her own survival was actually another woman's.

The life of a very poor man had turned in a blink of an eye to that one of a millionaire. God grants his worshipers and provides reasons for such grants.

End of Story

---

[3] Najat in Arabic means survival.

A Love Story in Madagascar

A successful trader is a smart one! Trade requires a man who seeks profits and avoids losses.

Abdullah is a jeweler, who is known for his outstanding successes. He focuses on certain countries where high incomes are made so that he can make a profit from there. He travels a lot between gold- and jewels-producing countries. He purchases mines in Africa; the last one he purchased is located in Madagascar. He travels on his own plane from one spot to another.

In his mansion located in one of the Kingdom of Saudi Arabia cities, his servants arrange his bags neatly and uniquely. Interestingly, Abdullah has some sort of an issue with even numbers. His whole life is managed according to odd numbers.

Once, his private lawyer living in Madagascar called him and asked him to fly there at once. Abdullah was on his plane travelling to Egypt for a recreation trip. Receiving such message, Abdullah turned the plane's compass toward Madagascar.

Abdullah's plane reached Madagascar and he was received by the lawyer at the airport. On their way, the lawyer told Abdullah that someone had shown up claiming partnership in the mine he had just purchased.

"Have not I always told you to make sure that no obstacles nor demands related the government of Madagascar exist?!" Abdullah yelled at his lawyer.

He asked the lawyer to contact that alleged partner and figure out who it could be. The lawyer contacted that partner, who came in a fancy car and pulled over at the hotel entrance. The valet hurried to get the car door open as a dazzling brunette came out of it.

The lawyer was taken by her beauty. He called Abdullah and told him that the partner was finally there. Abdullah asked the lawyer to get the hotel meeting room ready at once.

Abdullah entered the room to find a girl sitting and waiting for him. He looked down as he was impressed by her beauty.

"Emily Muhammad; born to a Madagascan mother and a Saudi father," she introduced herself.

Negotiations started between the two parties; however, they reached no agreement! Abdullah wanted to purchase the whole mine from the girl, who said that it was a family inheritance that she could not let go of. Actually, she had already let go of half of it.

Negotiations suspended and Abdullah asked for another meeting so that they could get back to it. Emily told the lawyer that she wanted Abdullah to come to her mansion alone that night. He thought about it for a while and eventually he agreed.

At that night, Abdullah prepared himself. He shaved, wore his fanciest perfume, and took the car to Emily's mansion. He reached his destination, where a sole mansion stood in the middle of a spacious area.

Now I know why she does not want to sell that mine. She is very rich and maybe she is seeking to get a higher price to sell, he wondered.

He reached the outer gate of the mansion that was opened for him to get inside. When he reached the inner gate, a servant hurried to help him get inside.

He was received by the servants, who offered him coffee. Later, Emily came downstairs to welcome her guest.

"Why do you want to purchase the whole mine? Why do not you want to have a partner?" she asked.

He told her that he wanted to control gold and jewels markets in the Middle East region.

"OK! I will give you the mine only under one condition," she said.

She was rich enough not to pursue money. She had servants and her beauty was unparalleled. However, she lacked a husband!

Her condition was that Abdullah would marry her so that she could waive the mine to him.

Abdullah was surprised by the condition. He expected it to be money, property, or anything but marriage. He did not see that coming!

"Take your time to think about it," she said.

They had dinner in the light of candles and started with casual talks away from life's burdens and passion for money.

Abdullah fell in love with the way the girl had talked as well as with her sense of hospitality. The date was over.

Abdullah left the mansion and kept thinking of the offer and the condition of Emily all the way to the hotel. Once he reached the hotel, he called her and told her that he agreed to her condition.

Emily was pleased! She laughed and told Abdullah that she would arrange for a marriage that would bring fairytales to mind.

In the morning, Abdulla woke up and called his lawyer to tell him that he was going to marry his partner. The lawyer was excited with that plan; however, Abdullah told him that it was not a plan. It was a marriage based on love.

The lawyer prepared the papers for the marriage to be conducted officially. Emily started preparing her mansion for marriage. She prepared dinner for this occasion and sent marriage cards for all those in Madagascar.

The Wedding Time...

In the ceremony that resembled *One Thousand and One Nights*, Emily showed up wearing an Indian sari adorned with magnificent charms. Abdullah arrived at the mansion in the company of his lawyer. Emily told Abdullah that she needed his personal ID, which he handed her. Later, she stepped into the mansion with a man.

Abdullah walked around the guests while introducing himself. Emily came out of the mansion and headed to the garden for the ceremony to start. The ceremony was over and guests left the place including Abdullah's lawyer, leaving the bride and the groom behind.

Through the mansion's garden, Abdullah and his wife walked under the moonlight surrounded by the cool breeze of the night. He talked as she listened to his sweet words of love and affection. She was taken by his charm. She loved him despite the fact that they had just met.

They went back to the mansion and headed to their bedroom. Abdullah was amazed by the size of the room as well as its contents.

Abdullah woke up in the morning to observe his beautiful wife sleeping next to him. He did not want to wake her up, so he went to have his coffee. Fifteen minutes later, he went back to the room and his wife was still asleep. This time, he wanted to wake her up, but that was too late! Emily died suffering from her fatal disease. It was her last night with the one she loved. Abdullah called his lawyer in tears telling him that his wife had died. Abdullah's lawyer called Emily's and both lawyers headed to the mansion. As all the servants were crying around, both lawyers met with Abdullah, who was cloaked by his deep sorrow.

Emily's lawyer told them that all her fortune had been transferred to Abdullah when she took his personal ID the night before.

Abdullah felt sorry for Emily's trust and kindness. He wished that she had told him about her disease earlier, but that time had now passed. This way, Emily's fortune was transferred to Abdullah, who established a charity under her name to help the poor and those in need.

End of Story

A Horseshoe

Prologue

Some people believe that bad luck exists in their own life; wherever they go, wherever they are!

Michael lived his humble life in one of the suburbs of Las Vegas; the city that never slept because of its gambling complexes and hotels.

This city is also known for having the biggest circus. Michael wanted to have some fun so he took a whole week off and borrowed some money from his boss.

He went to the nearest hotel to start gambling and turned all his money into chips of high values. He wandered around the casino till he found the right table to play poker.

Michael spotted an old man who had a large amount of chips that he had won in poker. He thought that it was a good sign and sat next to him.

"Hey there! Can I sit next to you?" Michael asked.

"Well, the place is not mine to tell you not to. Please do!" the old man replied.

Michael placed half of his chips to start gambling. The first card came out as an ace of spades followed by a king, a queen of spades and a jack. Michael wished his fifth card was a 10 so that he could get a royal flush and the amount of the bet.

At that point, the old man whispered in Michael's ears, "Your wish has been granted, but you need to pull out and feel satisfied with what you have made!"

Michael was surprised by the old man's whispers. Was he telling the truth or was he bluffing?

He waited till the poker dealer was done distributing cards and as the last one was coming down, Michael got his 10 of spades. He won!

Michael was filled with joy winning that round and getting such large amount of money.

But being a human, Michael became greedy.

He went back and bet all what he had, hoping to double it. Cards were distributed and with each card revealed, faces changed.

All his cards were losing…he lost all his money.

"Hey, where are you, old man?! You jinxed me! Why did you whisper into my ear?!" Michael shouted as his eyes were filled with tears.

"Why did not you force me to stop when I first won?" he continued.

Michael's week off was over as he was filled with worries and depression thinking about the way to get his boss's money back. He borrowed it more than once, but he was already jinxed by those words whispered to his ears.

A Tip:

Always be satisfied with what God has given you!

End of Story

Part One
Loved By a Girl Out of This World

Prologue

Man is always subject to dangers, but would we learn from our mistakes?

Nour Aldeen is a 21-year-old young man, who graduated recently from one of the Saudi schools with a very high score. He joined the Jordanian University and majored in medicine.

His family was proud of his achievement. Being accepted by the university, his father wanted to gift him something, so he went to the market to get him a proper gift.

The father bought a white cat with two different eye colors and a tail with a different color at its tip.

Nour was happy to received such a gift. He started to learn some tricks to pull with the cat; sometimes he taught her how to jump and to come to him when he called her name. He called her Sandra.

It seemed that the cat liked that name a lot; whenever he came to the house, he would call her and she would run to him to play.

Sandra grew up. She was three years old and became prettier than before.

On the thirteenth day of the month at midnight, Nour heard some noise coming from the dark kitchen. He wanted to figure out what was going on. So, he went out and saw

Sandra drinking milk from the fridge. He gently picked up the cat, brought her a bowl and poured milk in it.

As the cat was licking the milk, she thanked him. "Thank you, Nour Aldeen!" she said it clearly.

Nour froze! What had he just heard? Who said it? He turned around but could not find anyone but the cat.

"Maybe it's just my imagination. A cat does not talk!" He laughed.

Nour went to his bed and fell asleep in no time. Suddenly, the door was open, Sandra got in and went to his bed. She pulled the blanket and slept on his chest. Nour felt nothing but warmth and the cat loved him dearly.

The Next Morning...

Nour woke up and found that his breakfast was ready. He was so shocked that he did not touch it. He went to the university still thinking about who made the breakfast!

As lectures were finished, he went directly to his apartment. To his surprise, lunch was ready!

"Who is here?!" Nour shouted.

He went to kitchen and held up a sharp knife while shouting, "I said who is here?"

His voice echoed around the apartment as no one was really there but Sandra.

At night, as the moon was full, Nour had his dinner early so that he could get to bed. After brushing his teeth, he put the cat in her bed and headed to his room. Suddenly, Sandra got in. However, it was not the cat he knew; it was a beautiful human being that entered Nour's room while he was deeply sleeping. She approached his bed, pulled the blanket, and placed her head on his naked chest.

End of Part One

Part Two… What will happen to Nour Aldeen?

Part Two
Loved By a Girl Out of This World

Prologue

Sometimes, it is necessary to know about the hidden world…

Sandra laid down on Nour's naked chest. Gently, she placed her head lest he would sense her presence and wake up. She contemplated his face while drawing a wide smile on hers. She breathed in his breaths and smiled with love to each detail of his face.

Suddenly, she moved her hands down to his private parts. She wanted to feel him.

He woke up screaming, "Who? Where? What is going on?" he mumbled. He did not know what had happened. He looked right and left and saw no one but the cat!

He went back to sleep as his body was shaking in fear. Sandra stood up and took off her bra. She stuck her breast to his back. Suddenly, he felt warm and slept deeply.

The following morning, he was late for his lectures. He took the car and made it to the university, but he missed his first lecture. The lecturer did not allow him in, so he looked at his girl Rinad and winked.

He sat in the cafe waiting for his friend Rinad while drinking a Turkish coffee and eating a lotus cake. His hands were shaking because of what happened to him last night. The first lecture was over.

"Rinad, come over here!" he called.

He held her hands with his shaking ones.

"Calm down! What's wrong with you?" she held them.

He told her that things were happening in his apartment that he did not know who was responsible for.

She tried to calm him down and told him that she could go with him to the apartment after the lectures. They went to the apartment and got in. Immediately, Sandra jumped to welcome her love, who laughed and introduced his girlfriend Rinad.

"This is my girlfriend, Rinad."

The cat started to scratch the girlfriend's face, but Nour pulled Sandra away quickly.

"Why did you do that?!" he scolded Sandra.

He held Rinad's hands and sat her at the nearest chair. He brought the first aid box and placed some ointments and medicine to the scratches. Placing his hand on Rinad's cheek, Nour was about to kiss her. When their lips got closer, the cat jumped to attack Rinad while growling!

End of Part Two

What will happen to Nour's girlfriend?!

Part Three
Loved By a Girl Out of This World

Prologue

A loss is a piece of advice given to those who will not follow it!

After Sandra, the cat, had attacked Rinad and scratched her face, Rinad had to flee the scene. However, Sandra would not let her go. It jumped on Rinad's back and kept scratching her. Nour was trying to get hold of the cat, but it moved quickly that he could not control it. Nour asked Rinad to crawl. The cat stopped and Rinad ran away from the apartment. Nour followed her and held her hands to calm her down.

"Rinad, my love! Do not be scared. It's me…Nour," he said.

But, Rinad was almost out of consciousness; she could not hear him. He hugged her tightly and as she started to calm down, he sat her in the car and took her to the nearest cafe. They both were shaking in fear after that unexpected incident. Nour called on the waiter and ordered coffee for him and his girlfriend.

At night, after they both calmed down, they left the cafe. Under the moonlight as they walked among tree branches, they kissed while holding hands. At nine o'clock, Rinad asked

Nour to take her back home as it was getting late and her mother was bombarding her with calls.

They were holding hands all the way from the cafe to Rinad's house as they were listening to Fayrouz's songs as well as to soft music. They did not think much about that noon incident. Rinad forgot about the scratches she got from the cat.

Nour dropped Rinad at her house and went back to his apartment. He started looking for Sandra, but he could not find her anywhere.

Back to that noon incident, after Sandra had attacked Rinad, it followed her and went inside the car unnoticed. Sandra sat there watching them wherever they had been. She was listening to their conversations and burning with jealousy. Suddenly, the car stopped at Rinad's house. Sandra knew where Rinad lived and went after her.

At Midnight...

At Rinad's house, Sandra was looking for Rinad's room while being accompanied by three other cats. They located the room and immediately the four cats including Sandra turned into human beings!

What will happen to Rinad? What will the cats do to Nour's girlfriend?

Part Four
Loved By a Girl Out of This World

Prologue

We may seek to please others, but they know nothing about what lies in the hearts of those seeking to please them.

As the cats entered Rinad's room in their human forms, they directly attacked her while sleeping. One of them held her feet while the others held her hands and chest. Rinad was pinned.

Rinad tried to scream but all her attempts were in vain; her voice was muted as if she was suffering from sleeping paralysis, where one cannot move at all. It feels like one is pinned down by evil hands.

Rinad woke up, but she could not move her body at all. She found three women holding her hard and down while the fourth was standing at the end of the bed.

"What do you want from me? Who are you? What have I done to you?" Rinad screamed.

None of the girls answered Rinad's questions; however, Sandra approached her and spoke to her in words that no one knew of.

"What are saying? Who are you?" Rinad shouted.

"Rinad, the lover of the man I love, Nour Aldeen! How are your scratches doing? Have you forgotten about them that fast? Or were they healed by the hands of my love, Nour Aldeen?"

Rinad shouted as hard as she could, but it was in vain. Her mouth was covered and her voice was muted. Moreover, Sandra was terrifying as she kept reminding Rinad of that incident.

The three women started to tie Rinad closely with the ties brought from the underworld. They started to take off her clothes, even her underwear. Eventually, they stood up at the end of the bed waiting for Sandra's sentence to be executed. Sandra approached Rinad's ears and said, "What do you want your penalty to be so that you will not come close to my love anymore?"

How could Rinad reply with her muted voice and tied lips? Sandra laughed loudly and devilishly. She brought some ash out of her pocket and started to throw it over Rinad's naked body while mumbling few words. As she was done with that ritual, she approached Rinad's ears and whispered words that she would never forget. "You will never remember how Nour looks like. If he approaches you, you will see him as the devil, you will scream at his face and run away from him," Sandra said.

Later, Sandra ordered the girls to untie Rinad. The girls did as told…they obeyed their queen!

End of Part Four

Part Five
Loved By a Girl Out of This World

Prologue

Your heart is destined to fall for a certain person; however, that person may not be destined to be at your side!

After the four cats had attacked Rinad, executed their sentence, and untied her, Rinad woke up with a blank memory; she could not remember anything about the last night. All she could feel was pain in her hands, legs, and mouth along with some scratches covering her chest.

She did not know where these scratches came from. Rinad went downstairs and started to look for her mother.
"Mom, where are you? I'm late for lecture! Is breakfast ready? Mom, where are you?"
There was no response from the mother because she went out early that morning to run some errands for the house. Rinad realized that she had woken up late and missed her first two lectures already.

She called a cab and told the driver about her desire to reach the university as fast as possible.

At the University...

Nour started looking for Rinad in each lecture he attended, but she was not there. He called her house and her mother told him that Rinad went off to the university around one hour ago.

The third lecture was about to start as Rinad came in panting as she was running to get in before the lecturer would start. She made it and reached the room. Wrapping the lecture, Rinad went to the cafe and ordered some coffee to calm down and for a bite. Nour approached her and waved. She started to get more nervous.

Once he reached her table, she screamed, "A monkey in the university, A monkey. Help me!"

Nour was astonished as he wondered why would his girlfriend treat him that way! Rinad shut her eyes and opened them again to see a hairy creature with two horns hanging over his head. She saw him holding a knife and was about to attack her. She lost her consciousness. The university security guards called for an ambulance. They also arrested Nour and locked him in a room to be interrogated. The ambulance showed up and took Rinad to the hospital. As for Nour, the police came to the university to interrogate him.

The police could not find a reason to arrest him; he did not commit a felony or even was holding a gun!

Reaching the hospital, Rinad was carried to the room to receive medical treatment. The medical team could not find anything wrong with her except for those scratches over her face and hands.

"Where did you get these from?" the doctor pointed at the scratches.

However, she could not remember anything or where she got them from! Instantly, Nour hurried to the hospital to check on his girlfriend. Once he got there, he burst into the reception desk and asked about her. They guided Nour to her room (B13) as she was under medical observation.

He looked at her through the glass window. Opening her eyes, she imagined seeing a flame burning in the room hallway. She started to scream while pointing at the direction of the fire, which was actually the direction of her love.

Doctors and nurses hurried to her room and injected her with a tranquilizer that made her sleep at once.

End of Part Five

In Part Six

What is going on with my Rinad? Nour Aldeen kept asking himself.

In the following part we shall know.

What will Sandra do to Nour to make him forget about Rinad?

Part Six
Loved By a Girl Out of This World

Prologue

Death is a way to live happily ever after…

Nour came back from the hospital in a state of shock and confusion. He kept asking what could have happened to Rinad and why did she act like that!

He jumped into his car and headed to his apartment to find the one that was hiding for a whole day. Sandra was in the apartment facing a wall in a gesture that she was angry with him. He held her up and hugged her tightly. Immediately, she forgot everything.

"Do not leave me ever again! I love you!" Nour said.

Sandra lowered her head as if she was shy.

At night, Nour made dinner for himself and for Sandra. Finishing dinner, he called the hospital to check on his girlfriend, Rinad. They told him that she was still under intensive care.

Sandra heard the whole conversation and was burning out of jealousy. Suddenly, she disappeared. Nour could hear the door of the apartment shut. He went to check it out.

"Who is it?" he inquired.

No one answered.

Suddenly, his girlfriend, Rinad, showed up and hugged him tightly. She apologized for her actions in the university as well as in the hospital. He hugged her back and they kissed while holding hands.

"But, when did you come out of the hospital?" Nour asked.

"I just got out and came here," she replied.

She told him that she wanted to spend the night with him and that she did not want to get back to her mother's until tomorrow. Nour agreed immediately and made her bed, but she told him that she wanted to share his.

Getting ready to sleep, he caressed her to help her get rid of the stress she had been through all say. She was very submissive as if she was giving him the permission to do whatever he wished to. He did what she imagined he would do and they both slept, sharing a wide smile and a great relief.

In the Morning...

Nour woke up but could not find Rinad next to him. He kept receiving a call from Rinad's mother who called his mobile and landline. He was surprised to receive such calls at such early hours. He called her back to receive an unbelievable surprise. Rinad's mother told him that Rinad had passed away last night after a heart failure!

Rinad's heart was too fragile to handle all the shocks she had witnessed the day before at the university and the hospital.

Nour Aldeen was stunned as tears poured out of his eyes. Immediately, he thought about last night wondering who was the girl he spent the night with; the girl who shared his bed!

He burst into tears and started to talk to himself, "Who? How? What just happened? Why did it happen? Who was that girl I slept with last night? How did Rinad die in the hospital while she was sleeping next to me?"

Sandra seemed pretty happy as she jumped from one table to the other. She jumped over Nour, who was totally absorbed in his thoughts. He talked to the cat hoping that she might understand him. He told her that Rinad had passed away last night and he did not know how that happened; Rinad spent the night with him, but she died in the hospital!

Sandra laughed as she realized that she had no rivals anymore. The heart of the man she loved was now hers as the girl who loved him to death had already died. However, how could she tell him that he was hers and only hers?!!

End of Part Six

In the seventh part, Nour will know what is going on... But how?

Part Seven
Last Part
Loved By a Girl Out of This World

Prologue

We must let go of the past and accept our fates!

A month had passed since Rinad's death due to a heart failure. All that mattered to Nour was to know what had happened before the night of her death. He wanted to know who was the girl he spent that night with. He kept thinking thoroughly until he was fed up with thinking!

He wanted to take a walk in the market to get some winter clothes. Passing by an electronics shop, he found modern and developed devices inside.

He stepped in and was welcomed by the seller.

"How can I help you?" the seller said.

"I'm looking for something that I can use to record for long periods, day and night!" Nour explained.

The seller told him that they had advanced night cameras. He showed Nour many brands, but Nour approved one type called Orlo. It was a Korean camera that can be controlled through the mobile phone. Nour bought thirteen of them and the seller taught him how to use it and how to put it up without being noticed.

Nour started to install three cameras in the kitchen, another three in the living room, another set of three cameras in the hallway to his room, a single camera at the door of his room and another three inside his room. He linked all the cameras to his laptop as well as to his mobile phone. He tuned them in to record every movement in the apartment.

Nour went to the university but he was still thinking about Rinad right before each lecture he attended. He kept looking at the seat she used to fill. Sometimes he smiled and some other times he cried and grieved. He was waiting for this day to end so that he could go back to his apartment.

In His Apartment...

He hurried to his new device and kept running the records, but he could not find anything bizarre. The cat, Sandra, was moving right and left, jumping or playing with the ball. Nothing was in there but Sandra. Nothing strange could be detected.

He prepared his lunch and put some to Sandra that saw him drowning in his sadness.

"I have to make him happy tonight," Sandra decided.

At Night...

Sandra put on her human body. Softly, she moved to Nour's bedroom and opened the door. He was asleep as she approached his bed and started to hug him. Nour's erotic dreams with his love started.

Waking up, Nour saw the result of such dreams on his clothes. He felt ashamed and went to wash. During the shower, he kept thinking, *What is going on with me? Something must be happening to me when I go to sleep!*

He remembered the cameras and wanted to check them, but he was already late for the university that he had to leave without having his breakfast. He put Sandra's food carelessly and left.

He must be happy! Sandra thought.

As lectures wrapped up, Nour hurried to his apartment. Immediately, he got into the room to watch all the records. He could see a girl getting out from the back of the couches in the living room, but her face was not that clear. He followed her from one camera to another until she reached the camera installed at his bedroom door. Now, he could see her face clearly. It was Sandra the cat!

Nour stuttered. How did this happen? How could a cat turn into a girl?! He kept watching the records. He saw the girl getting into his room, approaching his bed, pulling the blanket, and sleeping in his arms!

Nour froze! He did not know what to do or what to say! He kept thinking about it but he had no idea how to get rid of that girl. He read old books, surfed the internet, and found many ways to get rid of the bizarre phenomenon!

He started with the Quran by turning on one of the channels airing Quran all day or by any other means. However, devices kept breaking down for no reason. He knew that he was all alone facing this situation.

He started to use holy water that had been blessed by readings from the Quran. He used salted water and white musk. He placed nets all over the apartment to catch the cat before it turned into a human being. In his room, he put a large collection of knives and inverted wooden crosses that had sharp tips.

He was ready waiting for Sandra's arrival. He prepared her food in the kitchen and left his clothes on the couch to show that he was in the house. The cat was happily eating her food because Nour did not forget about her. She smelled something, but all she cared about was how to pay Nour back!

Finishing her meal, Sandra turned into a human being. Calmly, she walked toward the bedroom. Stepping over the water Nour had splashed all over the apartment, Sandra's feet were burned; however, she could feel nothing. She was in a deep love that made her forget all the pains of the world. He heart leaped in joy and longing for her man. She entered the room to see Nour sleeping. She approached his bed and pulled off the blanket.

As she was pulling the blanket, Nour screamed at her face, "Die, you malicious creature!"

Nour stabbed her in the heart with a knife twice. Then, he used the inverted cross with the sharp tip to finish the job.

She was screaming, "No! Please, do not! I love you. I do not want to cause you any harm. Please!"

Nour kept stabbing her until she turned back to her normal image; a cat cut into pieces. Her eyes were fixed on Nour, the man she loved. She died looking at his face.

Finally, Nour Aldeen got rid of all his fears and all the bizarre phenomenon he had witnessed. He also took revenge for his love, Rinad!

End of Part Seven

The Man Who Killed My Love!

Prologue

A life shared with an honest soulmate that truly loves you is a life worth living...

Jamila was a librarian working alone in a spacious library. She lived a luxurious life with her husband Dr. Amr, who was a man of a weak personality. He did not love her nor their life as a married couple.

Meshaal was Jamila's childhood sweetheart.

The library was a place where many people went in and out for various reasons. Some people visited the library to borrow a book or to buy it. Companies too came in there to sell books. Jamila was stuck in that place; arranging new books and coordinating the old ones.

One Day...

Her childhood sweetheart stepped in. He was once a blond young boy with green eyes. Meshaal saw his girl standing there and could not stop all the wonderful memories they shared from pouring in.

He approached the front desk and greeted her. Smilingly, he reached out his hand, but she did not care much. She could not remember him; time had been generous enough to wipe the memory of the man she once loved.

"Do not you remember me?!" Meshaal asked.

She looked into his green eyes and suddenly she was hit by a stream of memories.

"Meshaal, darling!" she shouted.

"Jamila, darling! How are you? How is life treating after all these years?" he asked.

She wanted to answer that question, but out of respect for her marriage, she chose not to talk about it.

Meshaal left filled with hope that he could come back again to meet his sweetheart, Jamila.

On Friday, the thirteenth day of February, as rains were showering the city, Meshaal headed to the library to stand by its glass windows and steal a few looks of his sweetheart. He moved through all the windows to get a better look of her. She caught him and hurried out with a towel in her hand. Wrapping the towel around his drenched body, their eyes locked and their faces were close to one another.

Meshaal wanted to kiss her, but she opposed because she was a married woman. At that point, her husband stepped into the scene. Jamila tried to explain it, but jealousy and anger were already filling the air. Amr tried to attack Meshaal and Jamila stood in the middle to give Meshaal a chance to escape. Amr pushed her forcefully that she hit her head at the corner of the wooden table and bled before losing her consciousness. Amr and Meshaal started to fight, forgetting all about Jamila. The fight lasted for an hour, which was quite enough for Jamila to bleed till death. The library was covered in her blood.

Meshaal hurried hoping that he could save her, but it was too late. Jamila was dead. He held her head and whispered to her, "I have always loved you, darling! If only you had been mine forever!"

Amr received a life sentence and spent the following years of such life drowning in sorrow, regretting his crime.

As for Meshaal, he lived next to the grave of his sweetheart, strewing white roses and shedding tears of loss.

Moral:

Beauty comes from within. Appearances are mere means to attract eyes of lovers.

End of Story

My Thoughts and Words
Written by: Khalid Bin Khalifa Al-Qanbar
Your opinion is my motive.